Text and illustrations copyright © 2001 by Etienne Delessert

Published in 2000 by Creative Editions, 123 South Broad Street, Mankato, MN 56001 USA

Creative Editions is an imprint of The Creative Company. Designed by Rita Marshall.

Library of Congress Cataloging-in-Publication Data: Delessert, Etienne.

The seven dwarfs / by Etienne Delessert.   p. cm.   Summary: Stephane, one

of seven dwarf brothers living in the forest, relates how all their lives

were changed when they tried to rescue Snow White from

the murderous rage of her wicked stepmother.

ISBN 1-56846-139-9   [1. Fairy tales. 2. Folklore—Germany.]

I. Snow White and the seven dwarfs. II. Title.

PZ8.D3755 Se 2001   398.2'0943'02—dc21   00-043083

5 4 3

THE SEVEN
DWARFS

Etienne Delessert

Creative Editions

T-6314

  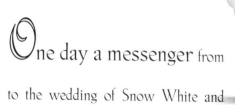

At the edge of the forest, there is a small cottage. It is not hard to find. Follow the sweet smell of wood smoke, and it will lead you along the hard beaten clay path to our door.

We've been living here for so many years now that we can't remember a time when we didn't. Work is hard. It is often cold in the cottage when we come home at night. We live like monks, tiny monks, to tell the truth. My name is Stephane, and my brothers are Ethan, Nathaniel, Achab, Samuel, Joseph and Solomon.

Some nights, when the house is so noisy with snoring and murmuring that I can't go to sleep, I look out the window at the moon. And I think about Snow White.

One day a messenger from the King arrived with an invitation to the wedding of Snow White and the Prince.

"What will we wear? We can't go dressed like this," Solomon complained nervously.

"It will be the King's pleasure to provide you the proper attire," said the messenger, before riding away on his horse. When the King's tailor was sent to our cottage with his three helpers, they took our measurements, up and down, and around the waist.

"You are . . . er . . . quite small, aren't you," stuttered the tailor. He was right. We *are* small. We discussed the fabrics, and after turning the pages of the leather-bound swatch book, we chose a splendid indigo velvet for the pants, jackets and hats. Later, my brothers and I went into the woods and caught a pheasant. We took its feathers to decorate our hats.

When the tailor returned with our new clothes, we could hardly recognize ourselves. "Well, l'habit fait le moine . . . ," he whispered, as he adjusted our feathers.

A few days before the wedding, three carriages arrived to take us to the Palace. The first one was decorated with fine sculptures and painted angels on the ceiling. It was wide enough for all of us to sit on the same leather seat. The second carriage was for our pig, King Henry. The goats and chickens rode in the third.

We had a superb trip through the countryside. All the villagers came out of their houses to stare as we passed. When we arrived at the Palace, the large gates of the outer walls opened wide for us. Our carriage stopped in front of a huge doorway, framed by rows of marble columns as tall as the highest trees in the forest.

"You're here!" cried a familiar voice. Rushing down the stairs toward us was Snow White, as beautiful and fresh as I remembered her.

"Welcome! Welcome to the Palace," proclaimed the King, accompanied by our friend.

"Oh, I'm so happy you could come," said Snow White as she hugged us, each in

turn. Prince Gabriel, her betrothed, a very tall young man, shook our hands firmly.

"Good to see you again," he said.

"Come on! Let me show you to your room," said Snow White. We followed her into the Palace, down long mirrored hallways that multiplied our images so many times we got lost in the counting. Our room was large enough to contain our entire cottage, and the bed was big enough for all my brothers and I to roll around on without even touching each other.

"Whee!" cried Achab, as he jumped up and down on the bed.

After we had unpacked, a valet knocked on the door and invited us to a light afternoon meal in our honor: savory cocoa sprinkled with sugar over buttered bread and some delicious marmalade of rose petals.

"How is your work in the mine?" asked Snow White, who had joined us.

"Cold," said Solomon. "Dark," added Nathaniel. "The same," I said.

"And the mushrooms? Are the mushrooms in the meadow still as delicious as I remember them?" she asked.

"Oh yes," I answered. "Just the same."

We then presented her with a box of our best shiny ore stones. There was polite applause from the ladies and gentlemen of the court.

"Aren't they charming, and so tiny," one woman exclaimed.

"Yes, so *marvelously* clever, and *so* small!" commented her companion.

That evening, while a choir of birds sang delicate melodies, a formal meal was served  on the terrace. We were given lace napkins and nervously looked around to see what other people did with them. When they laid them on their laps, we did too. Round, soft objects were served on finely sculpted china. We were told they were potatoes, a vegetable that came from a far away country called America.

After dinner, the Prince introduced us to what he called "cards"—rectangular pieces of paper, stamped with images of kings and queens, an invention that had come from China, he said. He showed us how to play—and the ladies and gentlemen of the court applauded again! It was fun to hold kings and queens in our hands.

"Well done, well done," the Prince laughed, and everyone nodded.

Over the next few days, we flew kites, swam in the pond, and played croquet, using mining hammers as our mallets. The Prince organized a circus for us, with monkeys, elephants and camels. Acrobats soared gracefully, and a magician changed huge monsters into hummingbirds. We had never seen anything like it.

Finally the day arrived for the King to officially receive us before his throne. All the dukes and lords of the Kingdom were in attendance. "Thank you for saving Snow White," the King began. "And for your service to my land

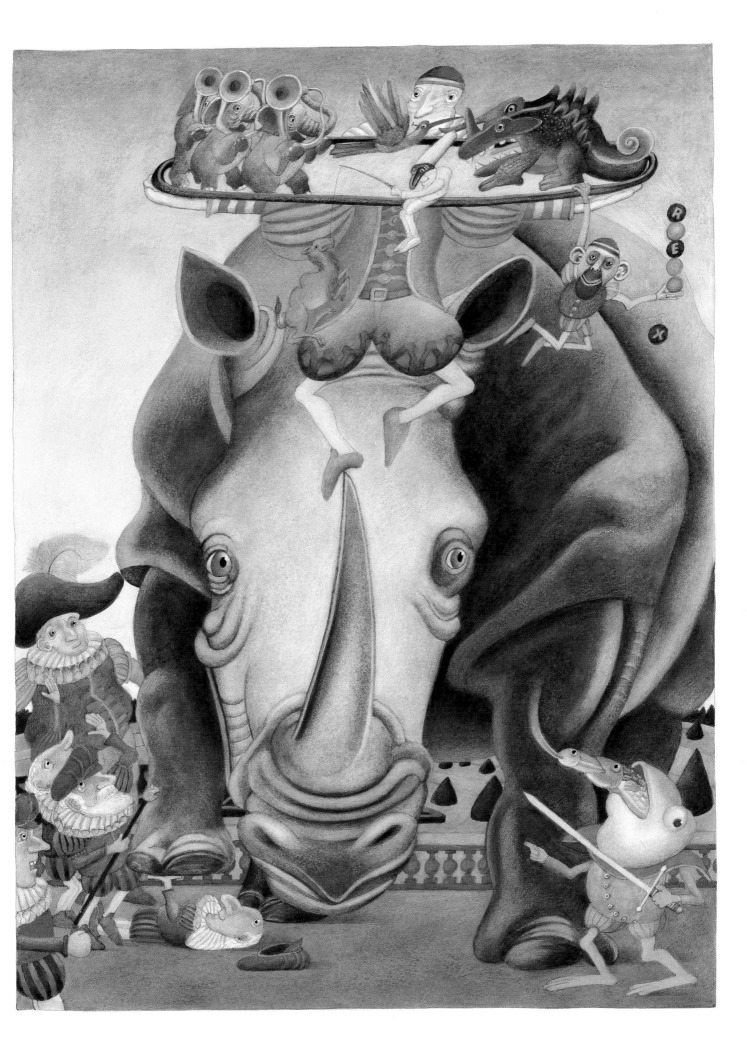

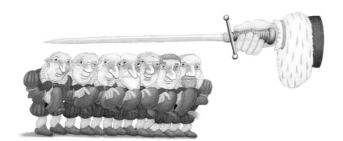

and people, we will be forever be grateful. In recognition of your noble deeds, I shall make all of you Dukes of the Forest." And with that, he hung shining gold medallions around our necks.

"It is my desire that you become part of my court," the King said, smiling broadly. "There is a cottage for you in the back garden, and if you like, you may be the masters of the royal forge! I would be pleased, little dukes, if you would teach me the secrets of the forest."

"Did you hear that?" whispered Nathaniel. "We get to stay in the Palace forever!"

"Thank you for the kind offer, Your Majesty. We shall consider it," I said.

There was a murmur of surprise and disapproval from the lords and dukes. Even some of my brothers were stunned as I looked up at the King's darkened face.

"As you wish," the King replied.

On the day before the wedding, we offered to select the flowers. We rode a golden carriage to the finest gardens of the Kingdom. We picked blue forget-me-nots and crinkled white peonies for Snow White's bouquet. Pleased with our collection, we carried the huge bundles of flowers back to the Palace. But just at the moment we arrived in the main hall, a tall waiter carrying a tray of wineglasses for the wedding reception glided around the corner towards us.

"Look out, Joseph!" I cried.

The waiter collided with Joseph, and the forget–me–nots went flying into the air.

"Help!" screamed the waiter, and Nathaniel grabbed his legs.

"I've got you!" shouted Nathaniel, but that caused the waiter to trip over the cham–bermaid, who was carrying an armful of linen. The maid fell against the sideboard, knocking over a fish bowl. All of this was too much for one of the King's monkeys who

 jumped up and down on the banister and clapped his hands.

Joseph was too embarrassed to speak. The chambermaid picked up the goldfish and rushed down the hall to find some water just as the King's chamberlain came on the scene.

"What's going on here?" he crowed. "You little people must stay out of the way. You are making nuisances of yourselves. We are very busy right now."

Exhausted by the day's events, we didn't feel like having supper. So we kissed Snow White good night and retired to our room.

I lay on that giant bed, wide awake. With the others asleep, I got up and went to the window to watch the swans on the pond below playing with the shimmering reflection

of the moon. I felt uneasy in the vast Palace.

Solomon stirred, then crawled out of bed and came to the window.

"Isn't it wonderful here?" he said. "And the food is good too. Listen, Stephane, we

should accept the King's offer and stay. I'm sick of the mine, and so are the others. Look

at these beautiful clothes! These soft beds!"

"Yes," I agreed, "it's a nice life."

"Stephane, it's a *perfect* life," Solomon replied as he put his hand on my shoulder.

I said nothing more and headed  back to bed. Eventually, I drifted off

to sleep, dreaming of the day we had met Snow White.

*J*t all began thirteen years ago. We had worked long hours deep in our

mine, searching for veins of iron and copper. The earth was rich in magnetite, a black

magnetic iron oxide. We broke the ore to size with hammers, washed it, and carried it

in leather bags to be sold to the blacksmiths at the forge. The blacksmiths would heat the

ore in the furnace, turning it into sponge iron. Then they would hammer it into knives,

tools, kettles and pots, or horseshoes, nails and hinges.

As I recall, that particular evening we set aside our hammers and pickaxes and

cleaned up in the cool stream. In single file, we followed Solomon, who was complaining as usual: "Look at me! I'm falling apart. I'm covered with bug bites." It was dark when we finally arrived at the clearing, but King Henry and the goats and chickens welcomed us with grunts, snorts and pecks. A blue jay flew from the fence of the pen toward the house. We froze—the door was ajar . . .

Holding our knives tightly, we entered the house. There was a candle lit on the table, and the shadows flickering on the wall made us shiver. No one. Nathaniel took the candle and led the way to the bedroom.

A young girl was found sleeping soundly on Samuel's bed! She must have been about seven, her face as white as snow, her cheeks the color of a pale rose, her hair on the pillow as black and shiny as limonite. She was the most beautiful child I had ever seen.

We stood in amazement, watching her sleep, then stole to the kitchen in silence and sat down together at the long table. There was not a word to be said until Solomon burst out, "Look, there's a mosquito! She could have at least closed the door."

We all decided that she could stay with us for the night. After preparing a meal of boiled cabbage, goat cheese and a loaf of coarse bread, we lay down on the hard kitchen floor and fell asleep listening to Solomon grumbling. We had heard it all before.

Early the next morning when we awoke, the young girl was standing in the kitchen

doorway watching us. Her once lovely clothes were torn and dirty. She had tears in her eyes as she tried a shy smile. "I'm sorry," she said. "I was so scared. I ran for miles through the forest. When I knocked at the door no one answered, so I came in to hide."

Ethan set an extra bowl on the table, and the girl sat down. She was just our size. Our little spoons were perfect for her hands, and our low dining room table seemed to have been built for her.

"Why were you running?" asked Joseph. "What were you afraid of?" Nathaniel whispered. "And what is your name?" asked Achab.

"I am Snow White," she answered.

"The Princess?" we all said in unison.

"You could have at least closed the door," grumbled Solomon. "Now we have a thousand bugs in the house."

Snow White wiped her tears. "Can I please, please stay for a few days? I'll sleep on the floor. I'll collect eggs for you. I'll do anything."

Then she told us that while her dear father, the King, had been away traveling, her stepmother had tried to have her killed.

"Why does the Queen hate you so much?" interrupted Nathaniel.

"Every day when she sits in front of her magic mirror she asks:

'Who is the most beautiful woman in the kingdom?'" whispered the girl. "The mirror always tells the Queen that *she* is the fairest in the land. But yesterday morning, I over-heard her ask:

Mirror, mirror on the wall,

Who is the fairest of them all?

And the mirror answered:

Queen, my Queen you were the fairest of all

But now I see Snow White is fairer still.

"The Queen became very angry and ordered one of her servants to take me to pick mushrooms in the forest. We rode for awhile and stopped at a large patch. When I turned to show the mushrooms to the huntsman, there he was, just behind me, with his long pointed knife!

"I was frightened and screamed," the girl continued. "The huntsman dropped his knife and burst into tears: 'I'm sorry, Snow White' he said. 'The Queen wants me to bring your heart back to prove that you are dead. But I just can't do it.

'You must run, run away, and never return to the castle. I will bring the Queen the heart of a deer and tell her that it is yours. Farewell.'

"So I ran away, until I found your cottage," Snow White continued. "Can I stay here for awhile?"

Agreeing that she could, we left for the mine. But what were we going to do with a little girl in our house? We were seven aging dwarfs with a set way of life. Now, a girl, the Princess no less, had come to us for help.

"If we don't help her, what will become of her?" asked Nathaniel.

"And she is small," said Achab. "She is really one of us."

As the days passed, Snow 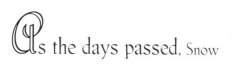 White made friends with King Henry, gathered eggs and mushrooms, and even tidied the house. Often she sat on the low bench, lost in her thoughts. We built her a nice bed of birch wood and put it in the kitchen close to the hearth. We spent our evenings around the table listening in the candlelight to her stories about the castle and memories of her father.

One day, we invited her to the mine. She wore one of my jackets, a pair of Joseph's pants, and tucked her long dark hair under Achab's hat. She no longer looked like a princess as she trooped along in her new disguise. Down in the tunnels she touched the raw, damp walls with her delicate hands, fascinated by this new world.

Back home, Samuel served everyone a glass of our raspberry syrup in honor of Snow White. It tasted better than ever. We talked and laughed until we saw the moon rise in the window.

$\mathcal{T}$he next day, returning home from the mine, we found Snow White dead; or so we thought when we saw our new friend lying on the floor.

"Quickly," I called the others to help. As I lifted her head, a tiny, golden comb fell from her hair. As she slowly opened her eyes, Ethan blurted out, "What happened?"

"A woman came to the door," Snow White murmured. "She knocked and called 'Lovely things for sale.' I didn't recognize her; she just looked like an old lady of the forest. She wanted to show me the beautiful ribbons she had in her bag. When I let her in, she offered me a small comb, which she put in my hair. Then I must have fainted," cried Snow White.

"That comb, the old witch poisoned it," exclaimed Samuel.

You must never open the door to a stranger again," I told Snow White as we car-ried the poor child to bed and laid her softly on a pillow of wild goose feathers.

Nathaniel and Ethan lit a fire to bake blueberry pies. Flour flew around the room. We were all very nervous. "It must have been the Queen," I said. "With our luck, she will close the mine," Solomon grumbled. "She might poison all our mushrooms. Or, even worse, she may come here and kill us all," he exclaimed.

I threw flour in his face.

The next morning, we got up and left for the mine, as usual. We are creatures of habit.

$\mathcal{M}$eanwhile, far away, the Queen sat in front of her mirror and asked again:

Mirror, mirror on the wall,

Who is now the fairest of them all?

And the mirror answered:

Queen, my Queen, you are the fairest that I see.

But deep in the forest, in the house of the seven dwarfs,

Snow White is alive and well,

And the child is the fairest of all!

The Queen trembled with rage. "I have killed her once. I will kill her again." Then

she dashed to a dark room in her turret where she sliced an apple in two, plunged half of

it into deadly poison, and glued it back together. When she had finished, she disguised

herself as a farmer's wife, jumped on her horse, and galloped to the forest.

Once again at our cottage, she knocked on the door. "Apples for sale," she cried.

"I'm not supposed to open," Snow White replied.

"But my apples are so juicy," said the velvety voice from outside the door.

"No, thank you," Snow White insisted.

"You are such a good girl to be so obedient," her stepmother purred. "I

will leave you an apple here, on the bench by the door, as a present, and I'll go away."

When we returned from our day's work, Snow White lay cold in the dust by the bench with a shiny apple in her hand.

We rushed her to bed and offered her water, but it was too late. This time she was really dead. We closed her eyes and decided to wait until morning to bury her. In silent vigil by her bedside, we wept throughout the night.

"But how can we bury her deep in the earth when she looks so fresh and beautiful?" Achab asked. "We must build her a silver and glass coffin, that way we can always look at her. She is still the fairest of them all."

So that is what we did. We placed the glass coffin close to the house in a bed of lavender and took turns bringing her wildflowers.

Her serene face and graceful body gave us the courage to continue our routine every day for the next thirteen years. We worked so diligently, we didn't even notice that inside the glass coffin, Snow White was slowly becoming a young woman.

One evening, as we returned from the mine, we heard the barking of a dog. A small band of hunters arrived at our clearing.

"May we have some water?" asked the tallest of them.

We offered them cake with their water and sat on the bench by the door.

"I am Prince Gabriel, from the Kingdom of the South," said the young man after he and his companions were refreshed. "Thank you for your hospitality. It shall not be forgotten."

The sun was setting through the dark green trees, and a ray of light tossed a luminous glow onto the coffin of Snow White. "But, who . . . who is this?" asked the Prince as he rose from the bench and peered in.

"She is so beautiful," he said, looking down. "She is the most beautiful woman I've ever seen."

"Alas, she is dead," I said, and told the Prince the story of Snow White.

 "My father told me of a beautiful vanished princess," said Gabriel, "and of the evil stepmother who killed her."

"The Princess's father has been broken hearted since the girl disappeared," the Prince continued. "He has searched his kingdom, tirelessly looking for some sign of her. With your permission, I would like to return her to her father's castle, so that he may be at peace."

Reluctantly, we agreed that Snow White should be returned to her home and to her father. We tied her coffin between two horses and rode with the hunters to the castle. But the trail was treacherous, covered with gnarled roots and sharp rocks. Along the way, one of the horses stumbled, and before our very eyes, the coffin slipped to the ground

and shattered, tumbling Snow White's body onto the forest floor. Instantly, the piece of poisoned apple that had been stuck in Snow White's throat dislodged and flew out of her mouth. Slowly, she opened her eyes. "Where am I?" she asked.

"She's alive," Gabriel shouted. "She's alive!"

With the help of the Prince, Snow White slowly rose to her feet.

"Look," whispered Achab in awe. "Look how tall she is."

When I awoke on the morning of the wedding, I knew we must return to our cottage in the forest.

"We will never belong here," I explained to my brothers as we dressed. "We will always be out of place in this world."

Although they did not want to admit it, they all knew it was true.

The wedding was a splendid affair. Snow White looked more lovely than ever, her black hair adorned with forget-me-nots and pearls, and the Prince wore a scarlet tunic with gold buttons. After the ceremony, we had a grand dinner with crystal glasses, hand-painted china and a marbled chocolate cake. The ball went on so late into the night that Ethan and Nathaniel fell asleep in their chairs.

In the morning, we thanked the King for his hospitality, but politely turned down his offer to stay. When Snow White learned of our decision, she asked, "But why?"

"The forest is where we belong," I said simply, taking her hand and kissing it.

"I'll come and visit you often," she promised, with tears on her cheeks.

"Yes, of course, you will," I reassured her.

We climbed into the carriage which brought us to the edge of the woods, a half mile from the house, where the road becomes a trail. Soldiers helped us carry our precious gifts. Nathaniel gathered a bouquet of white flowers. When we reached the cottage and sat down at the long narrow table, Achab lit a candle and Joseph served the wedding cake that Snow White had wrapped for us in large ginger leaves. A chipmunk raced under the chairs, looking for crumbs.

Stephane

Duke of the Forest

Autumn, 1613